I'M HAPPY THAT

_____

VISITS BERRYBROOK

Dedicated to God, who was always
at my side in creating this book.
And to my wife, Sherry,
who daily practices the virtues
portrayed in this book.

The Berrybrook Tales: The Big Race

ISBN 978-1-7340691-0-5

Published by Mignery Studio
www.MigneryStudio.com

Book Design & Editing by LaVonne Ewing, Image Resource

Somewhere out there is a place called Berrybrook. I don't know where, but I know it's there. It came to me in a dream, you see, but I saw no one there like you and me. Only happy creatures with smiling faces and each had homes in cozy places.

The path beneath my feet said, "Follow me, I have a treat!" It led me through bright flowered fields with chirping birds and bubbling brooks, past forests green and shady nooks, then said, "On you go and many fine folks you'll get to know!"

**The first on the path
I came to see was a
kindly rabbit named
Mr. Tweed.** He asked
all about me and my
friends where I live. He said,
"Friends of all kinds are good
for the mind and we all have
so much to give.

"You see, my friend Murray
the Marmot who lives next
door, shows me things I've not
seen before and the thing I do
for my friend Murray is calm
his mind of needless worry."

Then further on was Purrfina Felino,
tending her lawn in her purple gown.
One might guess she was going to
town, but it's just her way to dress each
day, no matter the job to be done.

Next door to her was a bird of
note, though under-adorned
in his shabby coat. But with
his nose in the air, he'll
make you aware,
**he is the great
Lord Featherwick!**

Most days in Berrybrook you'd find Lord Featherwick relaxed in his den, a book in one wing and in the other a pen.

Next door we'd see Elwood Weasel, working so hard painting his house or raking his yard.

These mischief-makers are good folks overall; Chicken Newdle and his pal, Lysall.

Later, in her beautiful shop
on Main Street in town, we'd find Purrfina Felino
still in her purple gown, selling elegant clothes
to the ladies around.

Now Bully the Bull, a farmer
by trade, would be found plowing
his fields in rows nice and straight.

Nearby, Felicia the Fox in the
shade of the trees, painting pictures
to sell and for others to see.

As for Mr. Tweed and Murray,
days were spent without hurry, on
the peaceful paths of Berrybrook.
As they walked, they talked of the
folks in this land, where they dwell
and how creatures so different
get along so well.

Now there in Berrybrook,
the days were all the same.
Those before and those
thereafter, each one filled
with fun and laughter.

Without hurry, just
like that, folks would
always stop and chat.
But this day things were
different; now a mighty
race was planned!

An invitation to compete went out to all the creatures in the land. Friends who used to stop and chat were busy getting rid of fat, in hopes of being first to place in this important race!

Alas, even Murray, who was not very fast, was doing his best to train, but he worried about his long-eared friend who felt no need to strain.

"But wait," he thought, "I nearly forgot! To train, rabbits have no need, because everyone knows they're made for speed!"

START HERE

At last the day of the race arrived, with all of Berrybrook coming alive.

There was Bosley the Beaver feeling quite proud, as he'd been picked from all the crowd to set the pace by starting the race with a swat of his tail on the village bell.

The great Lord Featherwick was ready to go,
flapping his wings to and fro.

Over there, Bully the Bull pounding his chest and
boasting to all that he was the best! "No need,"
he said, "for you all to begin, because I guess
you all know that I'm going to win!"

"Ho! Ho!" said Felicia
with a knowing grin,
**"you may find,
Mr. Bull, I
can outrun
the wind!"**

With a slap of his tail on the village bell, Bosley started a noisy stampede! To no one's surprise, Bully Bull took the lead.

"Wait, Wait!" said Mr. Tweed, "I must compliment Bosley on a fine job indeed!"

Murray cried, "Can't it wait 'til after the run?" But he stood quietly by until his good friend was done.

"Hurry! Hurry!" cheered Murray as they trotted away, "we can make up lost time and all will be fine!"

But alas a hurdle, poor Trotter the Turtle, flat on his back beside the track! Feet in the air, much in despair, carelessly bumped by the runners up there.

Now Mr. Tweed, in a kindly deed, lifted poor Trotter back to his feet.

And another gesture very nice, offered him this advice, "Four feet on the ground, good for balance all around, but if speed is what you're after, two legs will make you faster!"

"You're right!" yelled Trotter as he sped out of sight.

"Now," thought Murray, "away we go!"

But wouldn't you know, beside the walk
sat Gabby the Goat who loved to talk.
Gabby was known for the stories he
told, none of them new, all of them old.

He spoke of his youth; some with adventure,
some with some truth. Most folks he knew
gave a quick hello and hurried to go, but
not Mr. Tweed, the King of Kind Deeds!
Like everyone else, he'd heard them before,
**but he sat down and
listened once more**.

Over the hill,
past the mill, through
the stile, another mile.
All of this made Murray smile.
But another delay was on the way!

Down the trail they saw
Felicia the Fox with a
thorn in her paw.

"Oh yes, oh yes," said Mr. Tweed, "A tender foot this will impede. But I have right here just what I need!" With a tweezer in hand, the magic was done, and a grateful Felicia was ready to run!

"But wait! But wait!" called her long-eared friend, "Your foot must be sore, so my shoes I will lend." They didn't fit well, but worked for her anyway.

She smiled a "thank you" and darted away.

Now Mr. Tweed was
not the kind you'd find
without shoes any time.
So might you know,
he went quite slow
on tender feet over
twigs and stones.

**At last the
finish line in sight,** and poor Murray's fears were proven
right. Everyone was there and judge Purrfina had declared all
the winners in the race with Bully Bull in first place! Felicia Fox
was right behind and Elwood Weasel next in line.

Poor Murray was ashamed and hid his face, wishing he'd never entered the race.

But what he could not understand...

...was the happy face of his long-eared friend as he went from winner to winner, shaking their hands.

Bully the Bull,
Felicia the Fox,
Elwood, too,
felt so proud
as the
cheering
crowd
asked for
photos and
autographs.

They were also aware
they'd get to wear medals
at the party later that night.

**But for Murray
the party would
be no delight.**
He just wanted to
stay out of sight,
hidden for good,
and he probably
would, had not his
long-eared friend
asked him to attend
the party with him.

**That night
all of Berrybrook
came to show
their respect**
for the winners who stood so proud and erect as Bosley
placed medals around each of their necks.

AND NOW!

"And now," roared Bosley, **"The most important award is yet to come!"**

"What," gasped the crowd, "could be more important than what's been done?"

"I've been told of Mr. Tweed and Murray's deeds that put forth others' needs on the race path today," said Bosley.

"Now, we should all do our best at whatever we do and coming in first is a good thing, that's true. But Mr. Tweed and his friend Murray have shown us another way we can win.

"Putting others ahead is a great thing to do. Then others will do the same thing, too! So now listen to what I'm about to say, **I'm proclaiming this Mr. Tweed and Murray Day!"**

Our heroes were honored in a special way with a big parade the very next day. Everyone cheered with laughter and song and all of Berrybrook joined in the throng. Even Bully the Bull who had boasted so loud insisted on carrying our friends through the crowd.

Peaceful days were back again and Murray was proud of his kindly friend. His wisdom and thoughtful deeds are just what this world needs!

Suddenly the trees and the ground and flowers around began fading away and it was harder to hear what Mr. Tweed had to say.

Then soon Mr. Tweed and his friend disappeared
and in the last place they stood, my bedroom appeared.
As I awoke and found myself in my bed I remember the
last words Mr. Tweed said:

"Winning is a word that's hard to explain. Is it coming in first
or happiness gained? Happiness is not always at the finish
line. Sometimes it's trying to catch up from behind."

Someday I'll go back to Berrybrook when I fall asleep.
It's easy to do and you can, too. If you get there before I can,
tell Mr. Tweed I'll see him again!